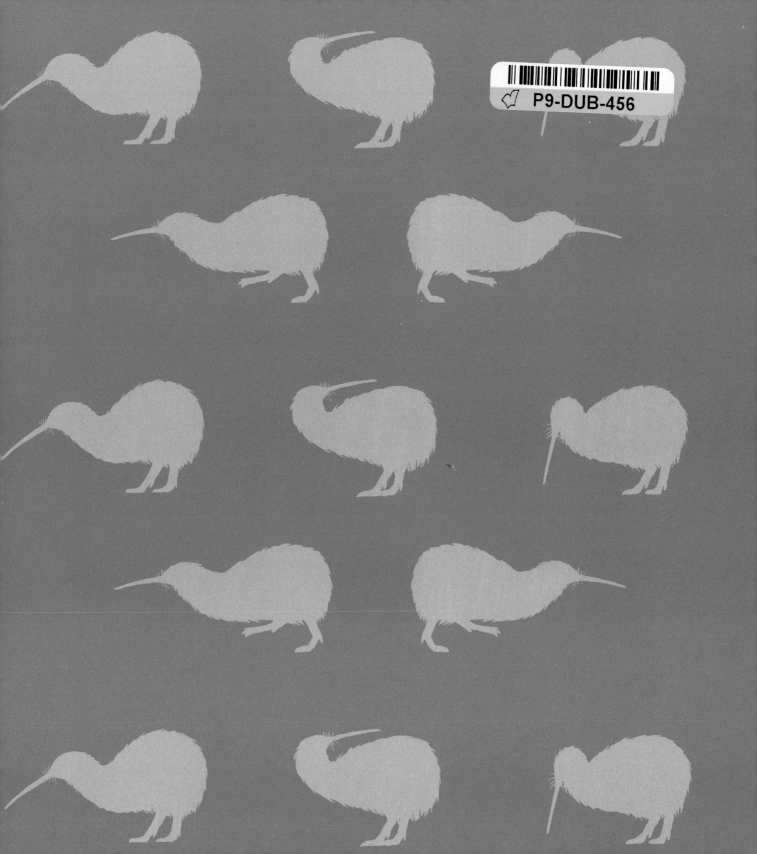

Established in 1907, Reed Publishing (NZ) Ltd
is New Zealand's largest book publisher, with over 300 titles in print.

For details on all these books visit our website:

www.reed.co.nz

Published by Reed Children's Books, an imprint of Reed Publishing (NZ) Ltd, 39 Rawene Road, Birkenhead, Auckland. Associated companies, branches and representatives throughout the world.

Text © 2002 Alwyn Owen
The author asserts his moral rights in this work

Illustrations by Dave Gunson

First published 2002
Reprinted 2003
ISBN 1 86948 715 X

Printed in New Zealand

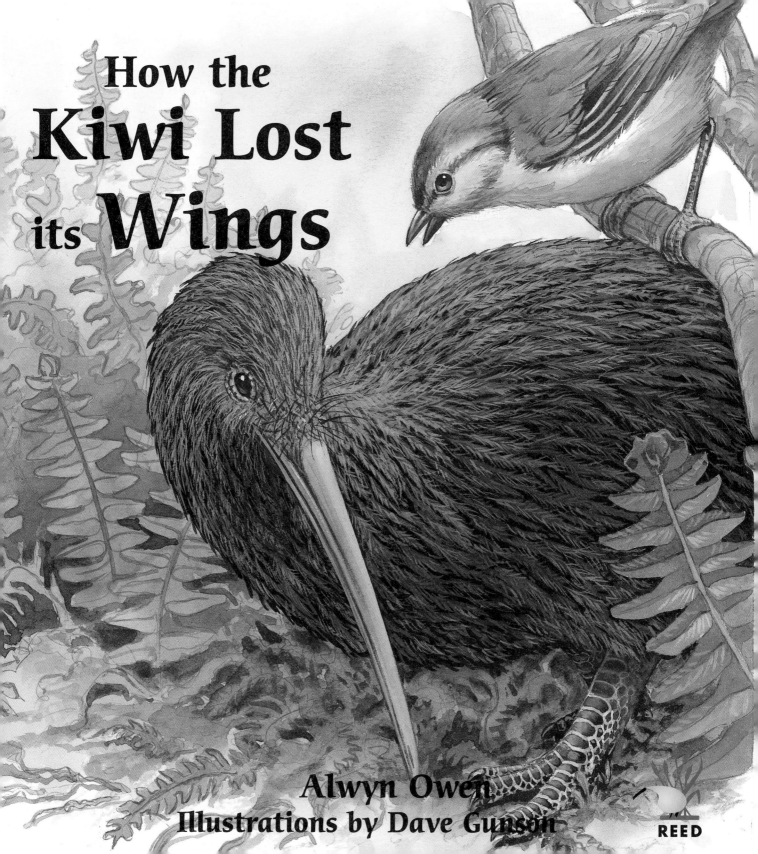

How the
Kiwi Lost
its Wings

Alwyn Owen
Illustrations by Dave Gunson

REED

*E*arly one morning, Puki the kiwi was creeping back to his little den under the old rata tree. He was very tired because he had been busy all night hunting for big juicy worms, and now he was looking forward to a long sleep in his warm, cosy nest.

In the trees above several birds were watching, and as they always did when they saw Puki walking, they said to each other what a shame it was that he couldn't fly. Riroriro, the grey warbler, flew down and said:

'Puki, I'm very sorry that you can't fly up in the trees like I can. Doesn't it make you sad?'

'No,' said Puki, 'not in the least. As a matter of fact, there was a time, long ago, when we kiwi could fly just as well as you can.'

'Goodness,' trilled the warbler, 'I didn't know that. May we hear about it?'

'Certainly,' answered Puki.

So all the birds gathered round, and Puki began his story.

Long, long ago — many hundreds of years ago in fact — the kiwi could fly as well as any other bird. But you must remember, friends, that it was a long time ago indeed, in fact not long after the great Maui had fished up this island from the depths of the ocean. There was much more forest in those days than there is now, and the God of the Forest was Tane Mahuta, the mighty Tane.

Now Tane loved the forest and the birds that lived in it. The birds themselves were very happy, and sang from morning to night. Many of those birds you would not recognise today: for instance Tui here had no little white bib on his throat, and Ruru the morepork wasn't brown as he is today, but was quite brightly coloured. And Kiwi? Well, as for us kiwi, we lived in the treetops like our friend Kaka here, and fed on berries, and nectar from the bush flowers, and instead of having brown and grey feathers, we were as brightly coloured as Pukeko is today. But remember, friends, this was a long time ago.

*T*ane was a father to the forest. He saw that the great kauri trees had room to grow tall and straight, and made sure that the young rimu saplings, with their beautiful drooping branches, had space around them. When the rain fell from the heavens and the wind threatened to blow down the great trees, he pleaded with Tawhirimatea, the God of the Great Winds, and the rain would cease and the winds drop, and the sun would shine again.

Then, one terrible summer, there was a great plague of insects, and the forest floor teemed with crawling, creeping things — beetles and centipedes and great wriggling worms. They attacked the trees, eating the bark and the leaves and the roots, until the bush was no longer green but a feverish sickly yellow.

So Tane called all the birds of the bush together, and they all came to him — Piwakawaka the fantail, Miromiro the tomtit, Morepork and Kaka, Pipiwharauroa the shining cuckoo, and every bird of every kind that lived in the bush.

And Tane said:

'Birds, you all know the terrible thing that has happened to our forest. Only you can save it.'

And the birds looked at one another and said:

'How? How can we save the bush, Tane?'

Tane answered them, 'Some of you must come down from the trees and live on the ground. You must forget the light and sunshine of the treetops, and live in the gloom of the forest floor. You must forget the sweet berries and the nectar of the flowers, and instead, eat these creeping things that are killing our forest. Which of you will do it?'

And none of the birds answered him.

So Tane spoke to Pipiwharauroa:

'Cuckoo, will you come down from the treetops and live on the forest floor?'

But the cuckoo hung her head and said, 'Great Tane, I am building my nest in the trees, and I cannot leave it to live on the ground.'

Then Tane asked the morepork:

'Ruru, will you come and live on the ground and end this plague for me?'

But the morepork looked the other way and answered, 'Great Tane, I love the light. The forest floor would be too dark for my eyes.'

So Tane spoke to Tui:

'Tui, will you do this thing for me and live on the floor of the bush?'

But Tui said, 'Great Tane, I am afraid. I do not know what enemies I should find on the ground. I cannot do it.'

The Tane enquired: 'Pukeko, surely you will come and live on the ground, will you not?'

But Pukeko said, 'Oh, Tane, the ground is cold and damp, and I like to keep my feet dry in the high branches of the trees. Besides, the other birds admire the colours of my fine blue breast and my red bill. I would miss the company of all my friends here if I left them to live on the forest floor. Perhaps some other bird will do this thing that you ask.'

So Tane spoke to Kiwi, the beautiful Kiwi who lived high in the branches of the tallest trees:

'Kiwi, will you do this thing for me?'

And because Kiwi loved the great forest itself even more than his life among the treetops he said, 'Yes, Tane. I will do it.'

Then Tane said, 'If you come down to the forest floor you must lose your bright colours and become grey as a shadow. You must lose your wings, so that in the long evenings when you sigh for your old life in the treetops, you cannot return there. And your slim legs must grow thick and strong, so that you can run quickly across the ground. Knowing these things, will you still come down and live on the forest floor?'

And Kiwi bowed his head and answered, 'Yes, Tane, I will.'

*T*urning to the other birds, Tane said, 'Kiwi of all the birds is not selfish. You others thought not of the forest, nor of the other birds, but only of yourselves. And so that you and all others will remember your selfishness, I shall change you all.

'Cuckoo, you told me that you were too busy building your nest to help. From this day on you shall never build another nest. Instead, you will lay your eggs in the nests of other birds, and they will scorn you.

'And Ruru the morepork — you who tell me you love the light. From now on you will live in the deepest parts of the forest, and fly only in the black of the night.'

'Tui — poor cowardly Tui who is too afraid to come and live on the ground. From this day you shall wear at your throat the mark of the coward — the white feather.

'And where is Pukeko, vain Pukeko, so proud of his bright colours? Pukeko who would not get his feet wet; Pukeko who loves the company of other birds. From now on, your feet shall know only the dampness of the swamps, and you shall live in the lonely places and spend your days far from the birds of the bush.

'But Kiwi — brave little Kiwi — though I must take away your wings and your bright feathers, your goodness will never be forgotten. In days to come you will be a symbol of this country, and those people who live here will be proud to take your name.

'And you other birds who would not offer to help me, you also I shall punish. I shall make you silent, and the voice of a bird will never be heard in the forest again.'

Then Tane looked up and saw Korimako the bellbird with tears in her eyes. And because he still loved the birds in spite of their selfishness he said, 'Korimako, you have touched my heart. I know what it means for you to sing, so I shall make my punishment less severe. Never again will the bush birds sing all day long as they do now. You will sing in full chorus only when the sun first touches the bush, so that each new day, you will remember.'

Then Tane was gone, and the birds flew away — Ruru to the darkest, most secret parts of the bush; Pukeko to the dismal swamp; Pipiwharauroa to search for a nest in which to lay her eggs. And Kiwi found himself on the ground, with the feathers that were once so bright now grey-brown like shadows. There was no trace of his beautiful wings, and his legs had become strong and thick, to scratch away the covering of dead leaves on the forest floor.

Tane had also given him a long beak to probe for worms and grubs, and a keen sense of smell and hearing to help him in his work.

And from that day to this, the birds haven't changed. Tui still wears his white feathers, and Pukeko still lives in the lonely swamps. And as you know, we kiwi still live on the ground and keep it clear of creeping things. So it has been for many thousands of years, and so it shall always be, for Tane himself ordered it.

His story told, Puki gave a great yawn and shuffled off home to sleep.

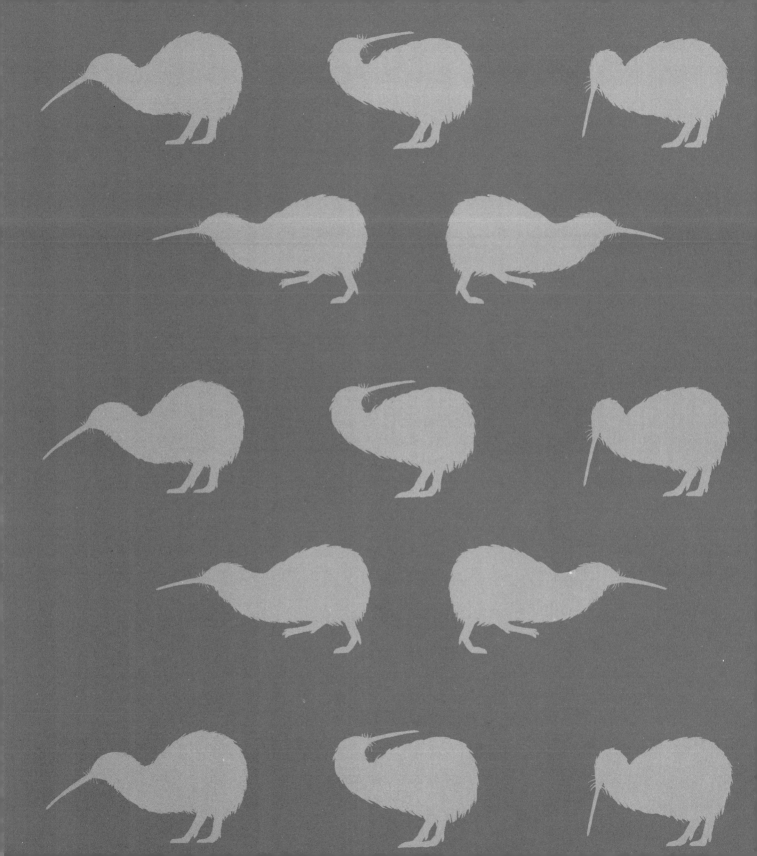